MICHAEL ROSEN

Aesop's Fables

Illustrations by

TALLEEN HACIKYAN

VANCOUVER ✦ LONDON

Dog and Wolf

Wolf was hungry and angry. He hadn't eaten for days and he was out on the prowl. It was night and the moon was up. All of a sudden he came on Dog. Dog was sleek and fat and jolly.

"You look well," said Wolf. "How come? Here's me, out hunting all night long and I'm starving. You look like you feed your face all hours of the day and night."

"Listen Wolf," said Dog, "you could eat like me if you did what I do."

"What do you do?" asked Wolf.

"I guard a house," said Dog. "I stop thieves and burglars from getting in."

"That's easy," said Wolf. "So if I do what you say, I get to eat like you do? Gobble, gobble, gobble, day and night?"

"That's it," said Dog.

"Right," said Wolf, "count me in. I'll join you."

Just then, Wolf noticed something round Dog's neck.

"What's that?" asked Wolf.

"Oh, nothing much," said Dog.

"No, really," said Wolf, "what is it?"

"Oh, it's just a little thing my master gave me."

"But what's it for?" asked Wolf.

"It's a collar. My master ties a chain to it and then he ties the chain to a post," said Dog.

"Why does he do that?" asked Wolf.

"So I don't run away."

Wolf thought hard and deep. "Keep your food and your job. I know I'm hungry but I'd rather be free than be a well-fed slave."

———◆———

MORAL *There's nothing more important than freedom. Even if you're promised a full belly, it shouldn't make you give up your freedom. Being a slave is worse than being hungry.*

Fox and Grapes

Fox could smell some delicious, sweet grapes. There they were, bulging and dark, nestling among the leaves. Fox could just imagine them bursting in his mouth, ripe and cool and juicy.

He trotted over to the plant and got ready to sink his teeth into the whole bunch. Up he went on his hind legs, up a bit more, up one little bit more … but, no, try as he might, he couldn't quite reach. He jumped, he hopped, he skipped, but it was no good. The beautiful grapes went on hanging there, just a little bit too high.

So Fox gave up and trotted off, saying to himself, 'Yeah, well, they were probably sour anyway.'

———◆———

MORAL *Don't fool yourself into saying that something is bad, when really you know it's good. You're probably only saying it because you can't have it.*

Crow and Fox

Crow found some cheese on a window sill, grabbed it in his beak, and flew up into his tree. Along came Fox who started up with his usual smooth talk.

"Oh wow! You are just about the most beautiful bird I have seen round here in years. I'm telling you, there can't be another bird as lovely as you—your colours, your shape, your personality. Look, believe me, you are one terrific bird. Do you know something? If you could sing like you look, you would definitely be the most seriously attractive bird ever . . . anywhere!"

Crow had never heard anything like this. He was so pleased and proud and full of himself.

'Me? Seriously attractive! That really is something,' he thought. 'Of course I can sing. Everyone knows crows have beautiful voices and mine is truly terrific.'

He made his chest swell out, took in a breath, opened his beak and—whoops! Out fell the cheese, down on to the ground.

Fox pounced on it, snapped his jaws round it and swallowed it quicker than a blink.

———————◆———————

MORAL *Don't get carried away when people tell you that you're brilliant or beautiful. They may be saying it just so they can get something from you.*

Lion, Fox and Wolf

Lion was old and sick and dying. One by one all the animals came to see him and pay their respects. They all came except Fox. So Wolf jumped in.

He was sitting all nicely-nicely by old Lion's side when he said, "My lord, have you noticed that everyone has come to see you, except one? And that's Fox. I'll tell you why he hasn't been to see you, it's because he doesn't care that you're dying."

Fox arrived just as Wolf was saying this. He heard it and then walked in. Old Lion was furious at him and roared.

"Hold it just there, my lord," said Fox. "Don't blame me only on what Wolf had to say. Where do you think I've been all this time? I've been here, there and everywhere looking for something, anything that will cure you of this terrible illness. And at last, I can announce here today, I have found it."

Lion was overjoyed. "You've found the cure. What is it?"

"What you have to do," said Fox, "is wear the skin of a wolf that has just been killed."

In a moment, Lion's friends set upon Wolf and skinned him alive.

———— ◆ ————

MORAL *If you plot and scheme against other people, you'll probably end up with them plotting against you.*

Wolf and Lamb

Lamb was drinking from a cool river. Along came Wolf.

"Hey, look out there, Lamb, you're muddying up the water. You're making it too dirty to drink."

"How can I be muddying up your water?" said Lamb. "I'm standing downstream from you. If I'm stirring up any mud, it won't come to you. All the water is flowing past you, then past me and away down the valley."

"Yes . . . well . . . anyway . . . last year you said my father was a fathead," said Wolf.

"That's impossible," said Lamb, "I wasn't alive last year. I was born this year."

"You know what your trouble is," said Wolf, "you think you've got an answer for everything. I don't care whether you're right or not. I'm going to eat you."

And he did.

◆

MORAL *People who are out to get you will come up with all kinds of excuses for bringing you down. But at the end of the day, they'll try and get you anyway.*

Mouse and Lion

Mouse was scampering to and fro, back and forth, fetch and carry; too busy to notice that he'd run over Lion's tail. Lion woke up with a roar and seized Mouse in his great paw.

He was just about to pop Mouse into his mouth, a tasty little nibble, when Mouse called out, "Don't eat me, Lion. If you let me go, I promise I'll do you a favour one day. Believe me, I will."

Lion roared out laughing. "You? A little scrap of a thing? You couldn't help a massive beast like me. Now off you go, you cheeky little critter, before I throw you down my throat."

Away ran Mouse.

Not long afterwards, Lion was caught in a trap. Hunters came and tied him up and went off for help. Lion roared and roared. The trees shook with the noise. Along came Mouse.

"I think I can help here," said Mouse. And he started to nibble and gnaw through the rope. It was long and it was tough, but in the end, Lion was free.

◆

MORAL *Even the strongest need the help of the weak. You're never too small or feeble to be useful.*

Frog and Bull

Frog was sitting in the river when he caught sight of Bull.

'What a creature!' he thought. 'What a size! It's bigger than a hundred frogs. I'm only as big as its eyeball. Oooh, how I would like to be as big as Bull.'

So then Frog started to take in great gulps of air. Bit by bit he began to swell up.

"Hey children, how am I doing? Am I as big as Bull?"

"No, not even close," they said.

So Frog took in more gulps of air. His skin was stretching like a balloon.

"How am I doing now, children?" said Frog. "Who's bigger now?"

"Bull," said the children.

Now Frog was really gulping. Gulp, gulp, gulp—in went the air and Frog was swelling bigger and bigger and bigger until there was a sudden bang.

Frog burst.

◆

MORAL *Don't try to puff yourself up and make yourself seem bigger or more important than you really are. If you do, you'll probably end up making a fool of yourself—or worse.*

Cockerel, Dog and Fox

Dog and Cockerel were good friends and they were strolling down the road together. When night came, they set about finding somewhere to sleep. Cockerel flew up into a tree, while Dog rolled around in a hollow in the ground down below. They each had a good sleep and when the sun started to appear in the sky, Cockerel stirred, threw back his head and let out a great *cock-a-doodle-doooo*!

Away in the woods, who should hear the noise, but Fox, and it wasn't long before he was there at the foot of the tree.

"Oh, is that you singing?" asked Fox. "I woke up this morning hearing such a heavenly sound, and I asked myself, 'What gorgeous creature can it be that makes such sweet music? I must find the beautiful beast right now or I'll hate myself for not looking for the rest of my days.' And then, what do you know, Cockerel, it's you! Come down, you wonderful bird, and let me shake the hand of the owner of the most beautiful voice ever heard."

"It will be a great pleasure," said Cockerel, "but why don't you come up and see me? All you have to do is wake up Doorman down there, get him to open the gate, and then come on up."

So Fox woke up Dog. And Dog snarled and snapped and tore Fox apart quicker than it takes a leaf to fall from a tree.

———◆———

MORAL *If someone stronger than yourself is attacking you, or if you think someone is trying to get the better of you with clever words, then go and get help from someone who can defend you.*

Mosquito, Lion and Spider

Mosquito flew over to Lion and said, "I'm not scared of you. You aren't any better than me. I suppose you think you've got strong claws that can scratch and sharp teeth that can bite—well, I know human children who can do the same. You want to know something? I'm stronger than you, and that's a fact. If you're ready, let's have a fight and I'll prove it."

Mosquito sounded his high-pitched hum, flew round Lion's head once and then landed on Lion's soft, hairless nostril. Straight-away, he pricked Lion's skin and sucked. The sting made Lion mad and he tried to rip Mosquito off his nose, but his great fearsome claws tore into his face. Again and again his claws scratched and ripped, but little Mosquito stayed on Lion's nose, stinging and stinging.

   In the end, Lion called out, "I give in, I give in. You win, you win. Now go away and leave me alone."

Off flew Mosquito, well pleased with himself. "What a feisty little fellow I am," he thought, "what a feisty little fell—"
   And floop! Mosquito flew straight into Spider's web and stuck there. Spider danced down the threads of the web, seized Mosquito in her jaws and swallowed him down nice and slow and easy.

—————◆—————

MORAL *Just because you outsmart someone stronger than you, doesn't mean that someone else won't outsmart you.*

Fir Tree and Thornbush

Down in the forest, Fir Tree and Thornbush were squabbling.

"'I am tall and beautiful,'" said Fir Tree. "I am useful for making houses and ships. You are a nothing-tree. A mean, low, prickly little thing, no good for anything except scratching children's hands. Don't even compare yourself to me. We shouldn't even be mentioned in the same breath."

"I agree," said Thornbush. "I am a nothing, and it's because you are so special that the axes and saws will be along soon to cut you down, while I will be alive and well years after you are hacked to pieces. Think about that, and you might find yourself wishing you were a thornbush."

———◆———

MORAL *People who boast and think they are better than others are often more vulnerable than those who are satisfied with just being ordinary.*

The Axe and the Trees

The people came to the forest and spoke to the trees.

"We have invented a very useful tool," said the people. "It is called an axe. To make it work we need some wood. We need wood to make a handle. Can you help us?"

The trees talked amongst themselves.

Finally, Beech Tree said, "We have talked about what you want and we have chosen Olive Tree. You need a tough, hard wood for the handle, and Olive Tree will be able to give you that."

So the people took the tough, hard wood of Olive Tree and fashioned it into a handle for their axe. Soon they were chopping away at the branches and trunks of all the other trees.

◆

MORAL *Sometimes the people who are most likely to harm you find ways to get you to help them.*

Partridge and the Fighting Cocks

Old Farmer caught a partridge and clipped its wings so that it couldn't fly away. He put it amongst the cockerels he was training for fights. Right away, the fighting cocks started tormenting Partridge, pecking at his legs, poking him with their claws and beating him away from the food Old Farmer put out for them all.

Partridge soon came to think of these birds as the most nasty, mean, unfriendly creatures he had ever met. He felt bitter and sad that he had ended up with such a horrible bunch.

But then he thought again. 'Look at them, these fine fighting birds, what do they do all day long? When they're not attacking me, they're squabbling and scratching at each other. Bicker, bicker, bicker—that's them. Small wonder, then, that when I turned up they picked on me.'

———◆———

MORAL *Don't take it personally when strangers are nasty to you. Some people are just mean and nasty, that's all.*

Town Mouse and Country Mouse

Country Mouse met Town Mouse in a field on the edge of town.

"Nice to see you, Town Mouse," said Country Mouse. "Why don't you come over to my place sometime for a visit?"

A few days later, Town Mouse trotted over to Country Mouse's house. But after a few days, he couldn't take any more.

"Listen, Country Mouse," he said, "you live like an ant. You eat really badly; little scraps of barley and oats. Why don't you come to my town house and I'll show you what real food is."

So Country Mouse followed Town Mouse into town and soon he was eating honey, dates, cake, peaches—it was a daily, delicious feast.

"Oh, Town Mouse," said Country Mouse, "you are living a real life here. Back in the country I'm not doing much more than scraping out the bottom of the barrel."

"What did I say?" said Town Mouse. "But come, sit down, I've just got hold of some beautiful pies."

Just as they sat down to eat, the door opened and huge human footsteps walked across the floor. The mice, terrified, scuttled down a hole. They waited, breathless, under the floor-boards until the footsteps moved off. Then, just as they came out of the hole, another huge human walked in. Off flew the mice again, under the floor.

"Look," said Country Mouse, "I can't take the strain of all this ducking and diving. I'd rather go on in my old hungry way. At least I don't have to be constantly watching to see if some gigantic horrible human is going to come in. I'm off, goodbye."

———◆———

MORAL *Being poor yet having peace of mind is better than being rich but scared, worried or in danger.*